YOU CAN BE ANYTHING!

YOU
CAN BE
ANYTHING!

Based on the comics by
Charles M. Schulz

RP|KIDS
PHILADELPHIA • LONDON

Printed in China

9 8 7 6 5 4 3 2 1
Digit on the right indicates the number of this printing

Library of Congress Control Number: 2008933259

ISBN 978-0-7624-3840-2

Text adapted by Megan E. Bryant
Art adapted by Tom Brannon
Design by Frances J. Soo Ping Chow

Running Press Kids
an imprint of Running Press Book Publishers
2300 Chestnut Street
Philadelphia, PA 19103-4371

Visit us on the web!
www.runningpress.com
www.Snoopy.com

Just like Snoopy, what you can achieve
is limited only by your imagination.
YOU CAN BE ANYTHING!

You can be a
LEADER...

Here's the
world famous

BEAGLE
SCOUT

leading his troop
on a hike.

Here's
BLACKBEAGLE
the world famous pirate,
leading his scurvy
band ashore.

You can be a
SPORTS
STAR...

And become a world famous
HOCKEY PLAYER

Or
JOE
SKATEBOARD

Or
A SURFER

Or a
BASEBALL
PLAYER

Or a
TENNIS PRO

Or you can become a
world famous
SKIER

Or a
BOWLER

Or a
GOLF PRO

Or a
SWIMMER

You can be a
HERO...

Here's the
WORLD WAR I
FLYING ACE
zooming through the air
searching for the Red Baron.

Here's
the world famous
FIRE FIGHTER.

Here's the
SECRET AGENT
carrying out his dangerous mission.

And here's the
FIRST BEAGLE
ON THE MOON!

CHOP
CHOP
CHOP

Here's the
RESCUE
HELICOPTER
on an important mission…

(the helicopter is
dangerously overloaded.)

Or you can
have a
CAREER...

Here's the world famous
LAWYER
leaving the courthouse.

Here's the world famous

GROCERY CLERK

working at the checkout counter…
(actually, there aren't more than a dozen
world-famous grocery clerks.)

Here's the world famous
SURGEON
on his way to the operating room.

And here's the world famous
LITERARY ACE.

Or you can
be just
PLAIN
COOL...

Here's

JOE COOL

hanging around
the student union.

SNOOPY ISN'T AFRAID
to try anything!

Here's
JOE PREPPY

And the
world famous
DISCO
DANCER

And the
world famous
ROLLER DERBY
STAR

Here's
PUNK
BEAGLE

And
JOE
GRUNGE

And
JOE BUNGEE

And here's...
FLASHBEAGLE!

Be a leader, be a hero, be smart,
and be different—because just like Snoopy,

YOU CAN BE ANYTHING!